Hanukkah

Festival of Lights

Celebrate with songs,
decorations, food, games, prayers, and traditions.

by Jeff O'Hare

Illustrated by Arthur Friedman
and Mary F. Rhinelander

Boyds Mills Press

For Sarah Gold Cogan, who taught us all we know, and for Sarah Taylor O'Hare, who taught us all we didn't know.
—J.O'H.

With special thanks to Lainie Blum-Cogan, Sandy Cogan, Sheldon Oberman, and Rabbi Alan Smith for all their help and ideas.

Copyright © 2000 by Boyds Mills Press
"It's Hanukkah" copyright 1994 by On Track Productions

Boyds Mills Press, Inc.
A Highlights Company
815 Church Street
Honesdale, Pennsylvania 18431
Printed in China

U.S. Cataloging-in-Publication Data
(Library of Congress Standards)

O'Hare, Jeff.
Hanukkah, festival of lights: prayers, crafts, recipes, games, puzzles, songs, and
more to explore the symbols and traditions for a joyous celebration/by Jeff O'Hare;
illustrated by Arthur Friedman and Mary F. Rhinelander.—1st ed.
[64] p. : col. ill.; cm.
Summary: Presents stories, songs, recipes, and activities related
to the celebration of Hanukkah.
ISBN: 1-56397-907-1
1. Hanukkah. I. Friedman, Arthur, ill. II. Rhinelander, Mary F., ill. III. Title.
296.4/35—21 2000 AC CIP
99-69851

First edition, 2000
Book designed by Randall F. Llewellyn
The text of this book is set in 13-point Berkeley.
The illustrations are done in watercolor dyes.

10 9 8 7 6 5 4 3 2 1

Contents

Introduction

Some may wonder how a person with a name like O'Hare could write a book about Hanukkah. Well, here's the story. My father, who had been raised a Catholic, converted to Judaism before he married my mother. Therefore, I was the product of a Jewish home. I was raised Jewish. I am Jewish.

You may think that some of the Jewish traditions might get lost or watered down in a house where one parent comes from a different background. Actually the opposite happened. Conversion is no easy process, and it isn't something to be entered into lightly. My dad was so anxious to learn all the customs and traditions that went along with Judaism that extra emphasis was placed on doing everything right.

When it comes to Hanukkah, I remember "snatching" latkes whenever my grandmother turned around to work at the stove in her small kitchen in Queens, New York. I remember lighting the Hanukkah candles and watching their reflection in the cold windowpanes. I remember my dad coming home to sit and read with us as the lights burned on. My mom taught us to play dreidel after dinner. I remember she somehow never won much, while my brother and I wound up with most of the gelt.

All in all, Hanukkah was always a time of great fun. I'm grateful for this opportunity to share some of the Hanukkah lore and games that filled our home on those candlelit nights.

When Is Hanukkah?

You can always count on Hanukkah to arrive sometime in late November or December, but why does the exact date change every year?

Actually, the date stays the same if you are using the Hebrew calendar. Hanukkah begins every year on the twenty-fifth day of the Hebrew month *Kislev*, which is the ninth month of the Hebrew year.

The Hebrew calendar is based on the moon's movement around the sun, so the length of the year is different from the length of a "regular" year. The Hebrew year has only 354 days instead of 365. Also, the lengths of the Hebrew months can change, and sometimes a whole extra month is added to the calendar. All of these things make the Hebrew dates match up differently every year with the days on the Gregorian calendar.

On the Hebrew calendar, a day begins at sundown. This means that the twenty-fifth day of *Kislev* actually begins at sundown the night before. Here is a list showing when the first night of Hanukkah falls for the next several years.

2000—December 21	**2007**—December 4	**2014**—December 16
2001—December 14	**2008**—December 21	**2015**—December 6
2002—November 29	**2009**—December 11	**2016**—December 24
2003—December 19	**2010**—December 1	**2017**—December 12
2004—December 7	**2011**—December 20	**2018**—December 2
2005—December 25	**2012**—December 8	**2019**—December 22
2006—December 15	**2013**—November 27	**2020**—December 10

Welcome to Hanukkah!

One nice part about seeing the days of late fall grow shorter and colder is knowing that Hanukkah, the festival of lights, is just around the corner. Soon there will be *dreidels* to spin, *latkes* to eat, and presents to open. *Hanukkiyahs*, or Hanukkah *menorahs*, will light up the windows, and songs will fill the air.

To what do we owe this special time of fun and games, candle lighting and gift giving?

Hanukkah is the celebration of a miracle that took place more than two thousand years ago. A powerful ruler named King Antiochus IV held the Jews prisoner in their own land for three years. Antiochus brought a huge army from Syria to destroy the Jewish religion and to force Jews to worship Greek gods. He took over Jerusalem and ruined the Holy Temple.

The Jews fought back, but they were outnumbered and might not have survived if they hadn't had Judah Maccabee on their side.

Judah Maccabee and his four brothers, who lived in the village of Modi'in, led a small, brave army against the Syrian forces. The Maccabees used their brains to fight the troops of Antiochus. One time the Maccabees built a fake camp and then hid away from it during the night. When the enemy came to attack the camp, the Jewish soldiers sneaked up from behind and defeated them.

Judah Maccabee and his troops finally won back the city of Jerusalem and freed the Jews, but the Temple was badly damaged. The Maccabees had to clean it up and make it pure again. They had to relight the special Menorah, a seven-branched oil lamp that was supposed to remain lit all the time. There was only enough oil left to burn in the Menorah for one day, but somehow it lasted for eight days, just long enough for a new supply to be made!

Finally, on the twenty-fifth day of the Hebrew month *Kislev*, in the year 165 B.C.E., the Temple was "rededicated," or made holy again. Judah Maccabee declared the day a holiday. The name of this holiday, Hanukkah, is the Hebrew word for "rededication."

The eight days of Hanukkah honor the eight days during which the oil burned in the Holy Lamp, and we light a special eight-branched menorah (plus one branch for the *shammash*) on each night to celebrate. This special menorah is called a *hanukkiyah*.

Every year in Israel, on the first night of Hanukkah, a special torch is lit in the town of Modi'in and carried by relay to a giant menorah in Tel Aviv. For Jews there and everywhere, Hanukkah is the celebration of a great miracle—not just the miracle of oil lasting for eight days, but the miracle of Jews surviving an enemy as powerful as Antiochus and every enemy who has followed since.

Hanukkah, which is observed during the month of Kislev on the Hebrew calendar, is considered a celebration of religious freedom. The menorah itself is a public display, letting everyone know that a house with a menorah is a Jewish home.

In comparison with most other Jewish holidays, Hanukkah has only a few symbols that are important to it. Some of the following sections will discuss each symbol individually, as well as include some new ideas on how to look at each of those symbols.

One of the purposes of these symbols is to serve as a reminder through the ages. The symbols make it easier to pass on the stories and vows of the ancient Jews to each new generation.

Where In The World?

The rededication of the Temple, which plays so big a part in the story of Hanukkah, took place in Jerusalem, a major city in what is today the country of Israel. Israel is located in the Middle East, near Egypt, where Asia and Africa meet at the Suez Canal.

More than two thousand years ago, the Greek Empire stretched throughout most of Asia. The Greeks were fierce warriors and mighty conquerors. King Antiochus IV, a native-born Assyrian, ruled in this part of the world. He was the one who tried to suppress the freedom of the Jews and tried to force the Jews to worship the Greek gods.

Today Israel is an independent country. There are still many conflicts between Israel and its neighbors. Other countries in this area include Syria, Lebanon, Jordan, Iraq, and Saudi Arabia.

On the right, the top map shows how the boundaries looked in the time of the Maccabees. The bottom map shows the current boundaries of various countries. Can you find Israel on each map?

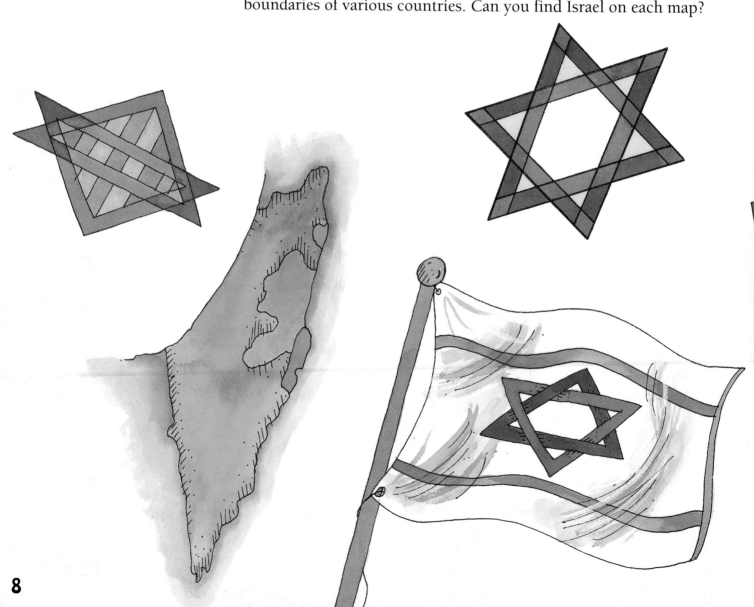

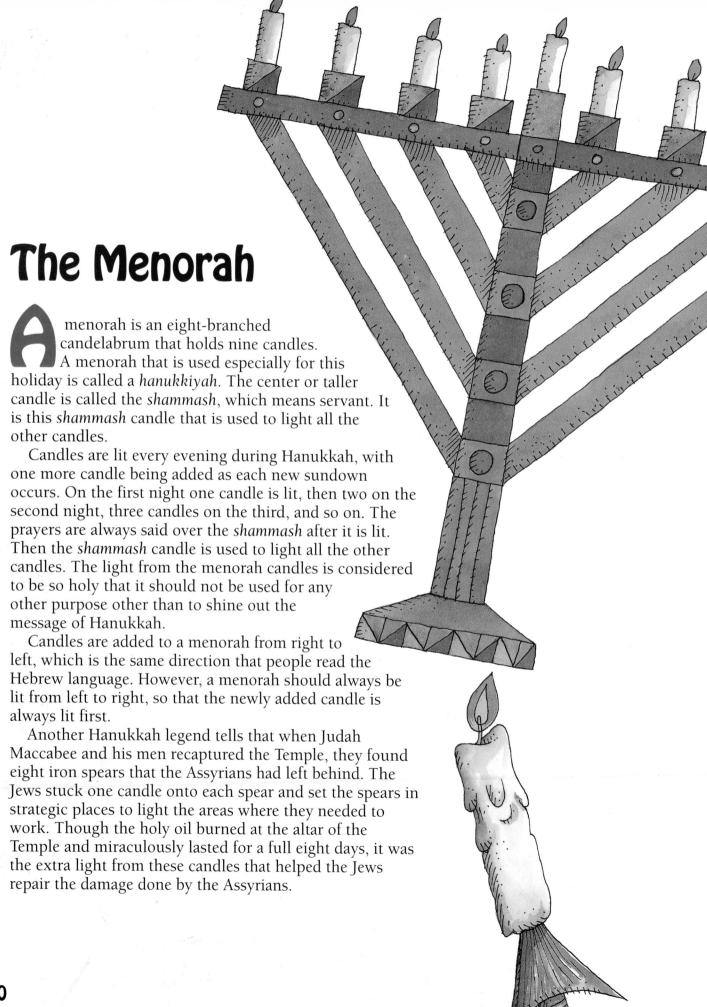

The Menorah

A menorah is an eight-branched candelabrum that holds nine candles. A menorah that is used especially for this holiday is called a *hanukkiyah*. The center or taller candle is called the *shammash*, which means servant. It is this *shammash* candle that is used to light all the other candles.

Candles are lit every evening during Hanukkah, with one more candle being added as each new sundown occurs. On the first night one candle is lit, then two on the second night, three candles on the third, and so on. The prayers are always said over the *shammash* after it is lit. Then the *shammash* candle is used to light all the other candles. The light from the menorah candles is considered to be so holy that it should not be used for any other purpose other than to shine out the message of Hanukkah.

Candles are added to a menorah from right to left, which is the same direction that people read the Hebrew language. However, a menorah should always be lit from left to right, so that the newly added candle is always lit first.

Another Hanukkah legend tells that when Judah Maccabee and his men recaptured the Temple, they found eight iron spears that the Assyrians had left behind. The Jews stuck one candle onto each spear and set the spears in strategic places to light the areas where they needed to work. Though the holy oil burned at the altar of the Temple and miraculously lasted for a full eight days, it was the extra light from these candles that helped the Jews repair the damage done by the Assyrians.

The Prayers

Each night of Hanukkah, families say the following blessings over the menorah:

Bah-rooch Ah-tah Ah-do-nai, Eh-lo-hay-noo, Meh-lehch ha-o-lahm, ah-sher kid-shah-noo bi-mits-vo-tahv, vi-tsee-vah-noo li-hahd-leek nayr shehl hah-noo-kah.

Blessed art thou, O Lord our God, ruler of the universe, who has sanctified us with his commandments and commanded us to kindle the Hanukkah lights.

Bah-rooch Ah-tah Ah-do-nai, Eh-lo-hay-noo, Meh-lehch ha-o-lahm, she-ah-sah nee-seem lah-ah-vo-tay-noo, bah-yah-meem hah-haym bahz-mahn hah-zeh.

Blessed art thou, O Lord our God, ruler of the universe, who performed miracles for our forefathers in those days, at this time.

One of the children in the household should light the menorah candles. A parent might lift the shammash first and then let the child use the *shammash* to light the other candles *(if he or she is old enough)*.

On the first night of Hanukkah, families also add the following prayer:

Bah-rooch Ah-tah Ah-do-nai, Eh-lo-hay-noo, Meh-lehch ha-o-lahm, sheh-heh-cheh-yah-noo, vi-kee-yi-mah-noo, vi-hee-gee-yah-noo lahz-mahn hah-zeh.

Blessed art thou, O Lord our God, ruler of the universe, who has granted us life, sustained us, and enabled us to reach this occasion.

DOUGH MENORAH

You need:

dough (1 cup flour, $\frac{1}{2}$ cup salt, $\frac{1}{2}$ cup water), a mixing bowl, blue and yellow food coloring, a cookie sheet, a Hanukkah candle

What to do:

1. Mix the flour, salt, and water together to make the dough. Knead it well until it is smooth. If the dough is too sticky, add more flour.

2. Divide the dough into two lumps. Add blue food coloring to one lump and yellow to the other.

3. Out of each lump, make five balls of dough about the same size. Flatten their bottoms.

4. Line up nine of the balls side by side on the cookie sheet, alternating blue and yellow. Press the sides together, using water to make them stick to each other. Put the last ball on top of the middle one to hold the *shammash*.

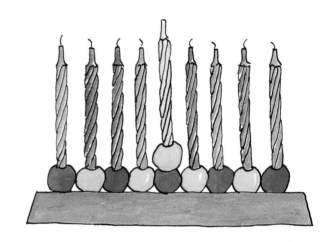

5. Use the Hanukkah candle to make a hole in each ball. Wiggle the candle around to make sure the hole is big enough and deep enough.

6. Have an adult help you bake your menorah in the oven at 300 degrees for 30 minutes. After you take it out, allow it to harden and cool completely.

7. You may want to cover your menorah with shellac after it has hardened. This will help to keep the dough from cracking or crumbling.

NOTE: Remember that your Hanukkah menorah should never be used for anything other than kindling the Hanukkah lights, and that candles and matches are to be used only with the help of an adult.

It is a Jewish custom to put your menorah near the window so that everyone who passes by may enjoy its warm and cheerful glow!

The Hebrew language is read from right to left. That is why you fill the Hanukkah menorah with candles from right to left. The candles should be lit, however, from left to right so that you are always lighting the newest candle first.

EGG-CARTON MENORAH

You need:

a cardboard or plastic-foam egg carton, heavy aluminum foil, scissors, 9 thumbtacks, glue

What to do:

1. Cut the lid off the egg carton. Cover the lid with aluminum foil. This will be the base.

2. Cut apart the cups of the egg carton. Trim off any edges or points to make ten even-size cups. Cover each cup with foil.

3. Take nine of the cups and push a tack up through the bottom of each one. (You will stick your candles on the tacks. Glue eight cups to the base, staggered as shown. Leave room at the end for the *shammash* holder.

4. To make the *shammash* holder, glue the bottom of the ninth cup to the bottom of the cup that has no tack. Glue the *shammash* holder onto the base.

NOTE: Before you push the candles onto the tacks, you may need to soften the bottoms so they do not crack. Have an adult help you heat them over a small flame to soften the wax.

FLAMELESS MENORAH

You will need:

a plastic-foam egg carton, construction paper (yellow, red, and orange), crayons, scissors

What to do:

1. Remove the top flap section from the egg carton. (Save this flap to make the dreidel craft on page xx.)

2. Cut off the top two cups. In the next row, cut off only one of the two cups. You should now have a carton with nine cups.

3. Cut out small flame shapes from the construction paper. By mixing the paper so that different colors appear together, you can make your flames look more realistic. You need at least nine shapes.

4. The single cup on top is now the *shammash*, so be sure to put a flame in that cup every night. Fill the remaining cups by adding one flame per day.

5. By attaching yarn at the top, you can hang this menorah on the wall.

REMEMBER: The *shammash* candle must always be taller than the other candles. If you hang the flameless menorah as shown, the *shammash* will stand taller. If you keep the menorah flat, you may want to add one or two extra egg cups to make the *shammash* taller.

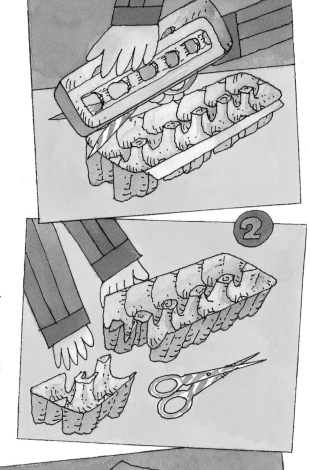

HAND-TO-HAND MENORAH

Here's a way to make a very personalized menorah.

You will need:

a large piece of construction paper, a pencil, aluminum foil or glitter

What to do:

1. Place your two hands on the construction paper, with the thumbs touching each other. Have a friend or adult trace around all eight of your fingers.

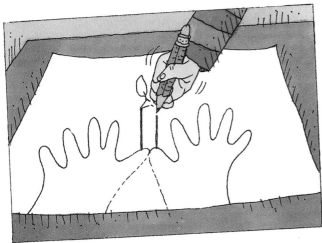

2. Draw one tall candle going up from the point where your thumbs met. You now have a menorah with a *shammash* and eight candles (your fingers).

3. Draw candle flames. Add pieces of foil or paper, or glue on some glitter.

4. Use a crayon or pencil to make a straight base for your menorah.

REMEMBER: Make the *shammash* taller than the other candles. Add a personal greeting if you want to share the menorah with a friend.

CAN MENORAH

You need:

8 small metal cans (such as the kind that soup or vegetables come in), 1 slightly larger can, aluminum foil, permanent markers, about 10 cups of sand

What to do:

1. Remove any labels from the cans. Then wash and dry the cans.

2. Cover the outside of each can with aluminum foil.

3. With the permanent markers, draw Hanukkah designs, such as stars and dreidels, on each can.

4. Line up the cans next to each other, with the big one at the end for the *shammash*.

5. Fill each can with sand. The candles will stand up in the sand.

SPECIAL MENORAH MATCHBOX

You need:

a small cardboard box with a lid, aluminum foil, fine-grain sandpaper, a small piece of felt, 6 matches, glue, scissors

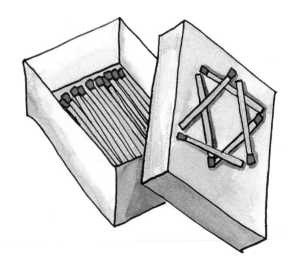

What to do:

1. Cover the outside of the box with aluminum foil. Do the same with the lid.

2. Cut a piece of felt to line the inside of the box and cut another to line the inside of the lid. Glue the felt to the insides of the box and lid.

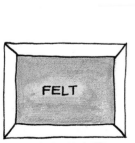

INSIDE LID

BOTTOM OF BOX

3. Glue a strip of sandpaper to the bottom of the box. Then have an adult help you glue the matches onto the lid in the shape of a Star of David.

4. Give your special matchbox to an adult to fill with matches and keep near your menorah, ready to kindle the Hanukkah lights!

FLAMELESS MENORAH

You need:

a piece of heavy cardboard (at least $8\frac{1}{2}$ by 11 inches), a piece of blue felt large enough to cover the cardboard, yellow felt, a ball of yarn or string, glue, scissors, a nail or pin

What to do:

1. Spread glue evenly over one side of the cardboard, and smooth the blue piece of felt across it. Make sure the felt completely covers the cardboard.

2. Glue pieces of yarn onto the felt to make the stem and branches of a menorah. Make the menorah any style you like. Just be sure it has nine branches, one taller than the rest.

3. With a nail or a pin, poke a hole in the top two corners of the cardboard. Tie the ends of a piece of yarn through each hole. Now you will be able to hang your menorah on the wall.

4. Cut nine flames from yellow felt. Each night you can "light" the menorah by putting up the correct number of flames. (The felt will stick to itself.) Keep the flames up until the next day to help you remember how many candles to light next.

Here is a great idea for someone who is too young to light his or her own candles. With this menorah, even the smallest child can take part in the ceremony without lighting a single match!

The Dreidel

No one is really sure where the dreidel comes from or how it became a part of the Hanukkah celebration. Originally, it may have been used by Jews who were studying the Torah when King Antiochus had forbidden such study. When the guards came around to inspect each home, the Jewish children would pretend to be playing with a toy. Others believe the dreidel may have come from an old German spinning top of medieval times that was adapted by Jews to remember the miracle of Hanukkah.

In most parts of the world, the dreidel carries the symbols *Nun*, *Gimel*, *Hay*, and *Shin*. These letters are supposed to represent the phrase *Nes Gadol Hayah Shem*, which translates to "a great miracle happened there." In Israel, instead of *Shin*, Jews use the letter *Pay*, which symbolizes the word *Po* (here), as in "a great miracle happened here."

Originally, the game was played with nuts as the betting tool, but you can use any object from coins to chocolates to raisins. The outcome of the game is pretty much left up to chance by the spin of the dreidel. There's not much strategy involved, but there is a lot of fun and laughter.

To play the game, just spin the dreidel and do whatever is shown on the side that lands faceup. Before the game begins, everyone should place three tokens (or whatever you're using) into the kitty. As the turns progress, everyone should put one token into the kitty when he or she spins.

If *Nun* comes up, the player does nothing. If *Gimel* comes up, the player wins the entire kitty. For *Hay*, the player wins half the kitty. If *Shin* appears, the player should put in three tokens, one for each of the branches on this letter.

Nun

Gimel

Hay

Shin

Po

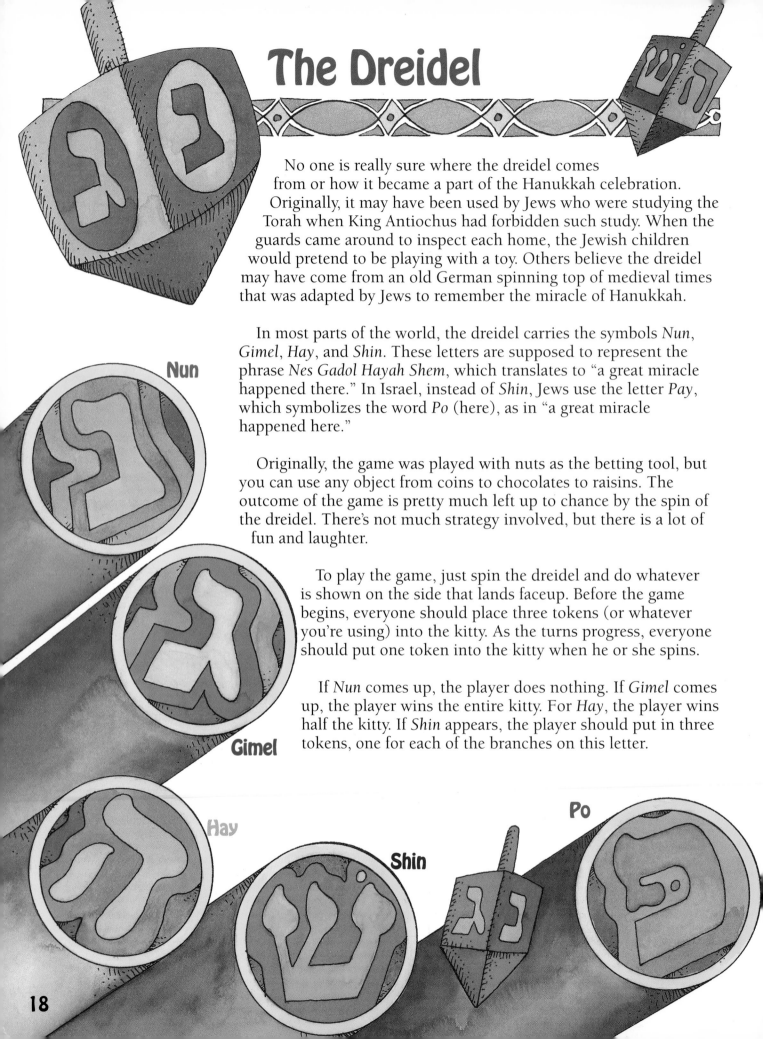

18

The dreidel has played an important part in Jewish history. There have been times when Jews were not allowed to practice their religion or study the Torah. They had to do these things in secret. Students would gather to study the religion but would keep a dreidel handy so they could pretend to be playing if soldiers came by.

DOUGH DREIDEL

What you need:

dough ($\frac{1}{2}$ cup flour, $\frac{1}{4}$ cup salt, $\frac{1}{4}$ cup water), a mixing bowl, food coloring, a cookie sheet, a marker

What to do:

1. Mix the flour, salt, and water together to make the dough. Add a few drops of food coloring. Knead the mixture well until it is smooth. If it is too dry, add more water. Be careful not to make it too soft, however, or it will not hold its shape.

2. Roll the dough into a ball. (First tear off a small piece to save for a handle.) Shape the ball into a cube by flattening the sides. Then shape the bottom into a point.

3. Make a small knob out of the extra piece of dough you saved and attach it to the top for the handle. Use water to make it stick.

4. Put your dreidel on the cookie sheet, and have an adult help you bake it in the oven at 300 degrees for 30 minutes. After it cools, use a marker to write the Hebrew letters *Nun*, *Gimel*, *Hay*, and *Shin* on it.

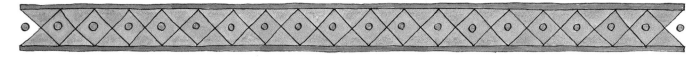

DREIDELS

◆ There are many ways to make your own dreidel, the four-sided spinning top that has become a favorite on Hanukkah among the young and old alike.

◆ Most dreidels have the Hebrew letters *Nun* נ, *Gimel* ג, *Hay* ה, and *Shin* שׁ on them. These letters stand for *Nes Gadol Hayah Sham*, which means "A Great Miracle Happened There."

◆ The letters also stand for Yiddish words that tell you how to play the dreidel game: *Nun*—"Nisht" (nothing), *Gimel*—"Gantz" (everything), *Hay*—"Halb" (half), and *Shin*—"Shtel" (put in).

◆ To play the game, start by giving each player a few "chips." (You may use raisins, stones, nuts, or any other kind of small object.) Put some of these in a pile in the middle. Then take turns spinning the dreidel. If it lands with the *Nun* facing up, the player does nothing. If it lands with the *Gimel* facing up, the player takes the whole pile from the middle. If it lands on *Hay*, the player takes half the pile, and if it lands on *Shin*, the player puts in one chip. Play until someone has won all the chips.

PENCIL-AND-CARDBOARD DREIDEL

You need:

a piece of cardboard (about 4 square inches), a sharpened pencil, a crayon or marker

What to do:

1. Draw two diagonal lines across the square, connecting the opposite corners. In the triangles, write the Hebrew letters *Nun*, *Gimel*, *Hay*, and *Shin*.

שׁ ה ג נ

2. Push the pencil through the middle of the cardboard. Your dreidel will spin on the pencil point.

CONSTRUCTION-PAPER DREIDEL

You need:

construction paper, a crayon or marker, scissors, a sharpened pencil

What to do:

1. Cut out a 4-inch-square of construction paper.

2. Make a dot in the center of the square. Fold in the corners to meet at the dot.

3. Write the Hebrew letters *Nun*, *Gimel*, *Hay*, and *Shin* on the folded sections.

4. Push the pencil through the middle of the square. Your dreidel will spin on the pencil point.

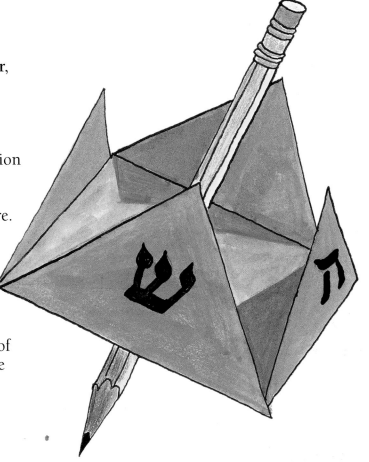

The dreidels that Jewish children in Israel play with have the Hebrew letter Peh פ *on them instead of a Shin. The Peh stands for the Hebrew word that means "here," because in Israel, Nes Gadol Hayah Po — "A great miracle happened here."*

OTHER DREIDELS

If you'd like to play dreidel but don't have one of the tops handy, here's one way to play the same game.

You will need:

a plastic-foam egg carton, a small bag or box, a pen or permanent marker

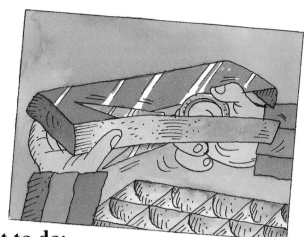

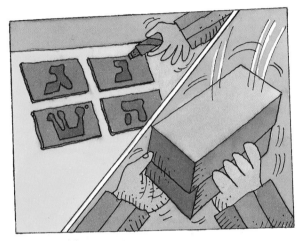

What to do:

1. Cut off the top of the egg carton. (If you want, save the bottom section for the menorah on page 14.) Cut off the edges from the top so that you're left with a flat piece of plastic foam.

2. Cut this plastic foam into four pieces of the same size. Mark each title with one of the different letters that appear on a dreidel (*Nun, Gimel, Hay, Shin*). Place these four tiles in the bag or box. Close it and shake.

3. Each player picks one of the tiles and takes the appropriate action. The player then replaces the tile in the bag and the next player picks. Use the same rules as in a regular game of dreidel.

This dreidel game works well in the car or in places where all the floors are covered with rugs.

Also, you can use four different-colored objects such as marbles or crayons. Be sure to mark each object with one of the four symbols from the dreidel. Then put these objects in a bag. Each player draws one object out of the bag. Use the same rules as in a regular game of dreidel.

MACCABEE DREIDELS

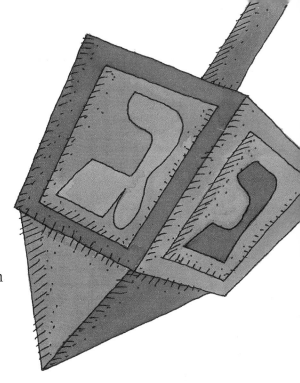

For 2 or more players. Each person must have his or her own dreidel. This game can be played in one round, or for the highest points in a number of rounds.

Each player spins a dreidel. The dreidels should be spun in close proximity so they will bump into one another. The dreidel that falls down first after a collision loses that round. If both dreidels fall, the one with the higher letter faceup is the winner. The order for this should be the same as in the dreidel game — *Nun*, *Gimel*, *Hay*, and *Shin* (with Shin being the highest). If all the dreidels have the same letter faceup, it's a tie. No one wins that round.

OTHER DREIDEL GAMES

Another way to incorporate the dreidel into almost any game is to use it like a die. When you toss the dreidel beside a game, use the letters to determine whether you move one, two, three, or four spaces. Or check page 30 for another way to use your dreidel.

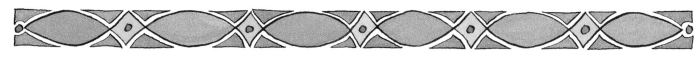

MACCABEE BOWLING

One of the most important parts of the original celebration of Hanukkah was Judah Maccabee's battle to regain the Holy Temple in the city of Jerusalem. You can play Maccabee Bowling for a fun version of this struggle.

You will need:

six or ten empty half-gallon milk containers or 1-liter beverage bottles, construction paper ($8\frac{1}{2}$" by 11"), permanent markers, glue or tape, a rubber ball or newspaper

What to do:

1. On construction paper, draw a picture of a big, scary face. Spread glue on the front and sides of one milk container. Glue down the face as shown. If you don't have glue, tape the face in place at the sides. Repeat until all of the containers have a scary face on them.

2. Arrange the containers on the floor in a triangle shape.

3. Take six to ten steps away from the front of the triangle. Roll the ball at the containers, scoring one point for every one you knock over. Just as in regular bowling, you get two tries to knock over all the containers. Every two tries is called a frame. Then you have to set up the containers and try again, or let the next person take a turn. Add up the scores after ten frames and see who knocked over the most "pins."

4. If you don't have a ball, wad a few pages of newspaper into the shape of a softball. Tape the papers in place when the ball is the size you want.

This game works best on a wood or tile floor. The ball won't roll as easily on thick carpet. **If you're playing in the house, watch out for tables, lamps, and other objects.**

EIGHT CANDLES MATCH-UP

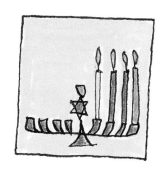

You need:

4 pieces of cardboard (each about 8 square inches), construction paper, scissors, crayons or markers, a ruler

What to do:

1. Use the ruler to draw two lines down and two lines across each piece of cardboard, making nine even squares on each card.

2. Draw a Star of David in the center square of each card. Write the numbers 1 through 8 in the other squares.

3. Cut 32 squares of construction paper, about the same size as the squares on the cards. On four of the pieces of paper, draw a Hanukkah menorah with one candle lit. On four more, draw a menorah with two candles lit. On another four, draw a menorah with three candles lit, and so on.

How to play:

Up to four people can play this game.

Give each player a numbered card. Spread the paper squares facedown in the middle of the table.

Take turns choosing squares from the middle. Match the number of candles with a number on your card. Put the paper squares over the numbers that they match. If you pick a square with a number you already have, return the square facedown to the middle and give the next player his or her turn. The first person to fill up a card is the winner.

FLIP THE LATKE!

You need:

a small paper plate, an ice-cream stick, string or yarn (about 2 feet long), a piece of heavy cardboard, scissors, crayons or markers, glue

What to do:

1. Glue one end of the ice-cream stick to the paper plate to make a "frying pan." Color the frying pan with crayons or markers if you wish.

2. Poke a hole near the edge of the plate, and tie one end of the string through it.

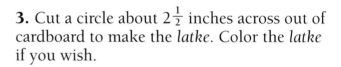

3. Cut a circle about $2\frac{1}{2}$ inches across out of cardboard to make the *latke*. Color the *latke* if you wish.

4. Poke a hole through the edge of the *latke* and tie the other end of the string to it.

How to play:

◆ Try to flip the *latke* onto the pan. See how many times in a row you can make the *latke* land in the pan.

◆ Have a contest with a friend to see who can flip the *latke* into the pan the most times in one minute.

No one knows exactly why we eat latkes, *or potato pancakes, on Hanukkah, but many people believe it is because they are made with oil and help us to celebrate the miracle of the oil that burned in the Temple for eight days.*

LATKE TOSS

Use a wastebasket as a target. If you don't have a wastebasket, draw a circle about 1 foot in diameter on a piece of cardboard. Collect as many small plastic lids from butter or margarine tubs as you can find. Mark off at least 5 feet between you and the target. Now see how many of the plastic "*latkes*" you can flip into the target "plate." The person with the most latkes on his or her plate after three tries is the winner.

Remember, this is just a game, and you shouldn't try this with real *latkes*.

A DROP IN THE BUCKET

This is a good way to learn about *Tzedekah*, or charity, which should be practiced all year but is especially important during Hanukkah.

Get five pieces of your Hanukkah *gelt*. Use real money or chocolate coins. You'll also need a ruler and a large can. Remove the top from the can. Ask a grown-up to place masking tape over the rim so there will be no sharp edges.

Place a coin on one end of the ruler while you hold on the other end. Stand up straight and extend your arm in front of you. Hold the end of the ruler over the can. Try to tip the coin into the can. Once you are skilled at one coin, try for two at the same time, then three, then four, until you can finally tip in all five coins at the same time. The player with the highest number of coins landing in the can after three tries wins.

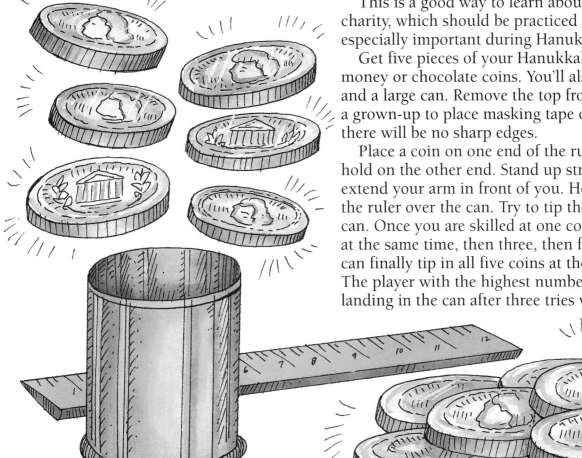

27

PIN THE CANDLE ON THE MENORAH

You need:

a large piece of white paper, a crayon or marker, colored construction paper, scissors, tape, a blindfold

What to do:

1. Draw a large menorah on the white paper. Write the word *shammash* on the tallest candleholder. Write the numbers 1 through 8 on the other candleholders, going from right to left.

2. Cut nine candles out of construction paper. Label one of them the *shammash* and number the others 1 through 8.

How to play:

◆ Hang the menorah on a wall where everyone can reach it.
◆ Give each player a candle with a piece of tape on the back.
◆ Each player is blindfolded and sent toward the menorah to try to tape his or her candle to the correct holder. The person whose candle comes closest to its holder is the winner.

MACCABEE CHECKERS

This is a game for two players. One player represents the Maccabees and the other player represents the Assyrians.

Each player uses only nine checkers, which are placed in the corners as shown. The checkers are placed only on the dark squares.

Each piece may one square at a time, diagonally forward onto another dark square. Normal pieces may not move backward. A piece may jump (and capture) only an opponent's piece.

If a piece reaches the opponent's far corner, that piece becomes a King. Kings may move and jump in any direction.

The winner of the game is the one who captures all of the opponent's pieces.

TO THE TEMPLE

The object of this game is to be the first one to reach the Holy Temple in Jerusalem. Use your dreidel to determine the number of spaces you can move by referring to the chart below. When you land on a space, do whatever it tells you. If one space sends you to a second space, DO NOT do what it says on the second space. Just remain there until your next turn.

Nun—No move
Gimel—Move ahead two spaces
Hay—Go back one
Shin—Move ahead three spaces

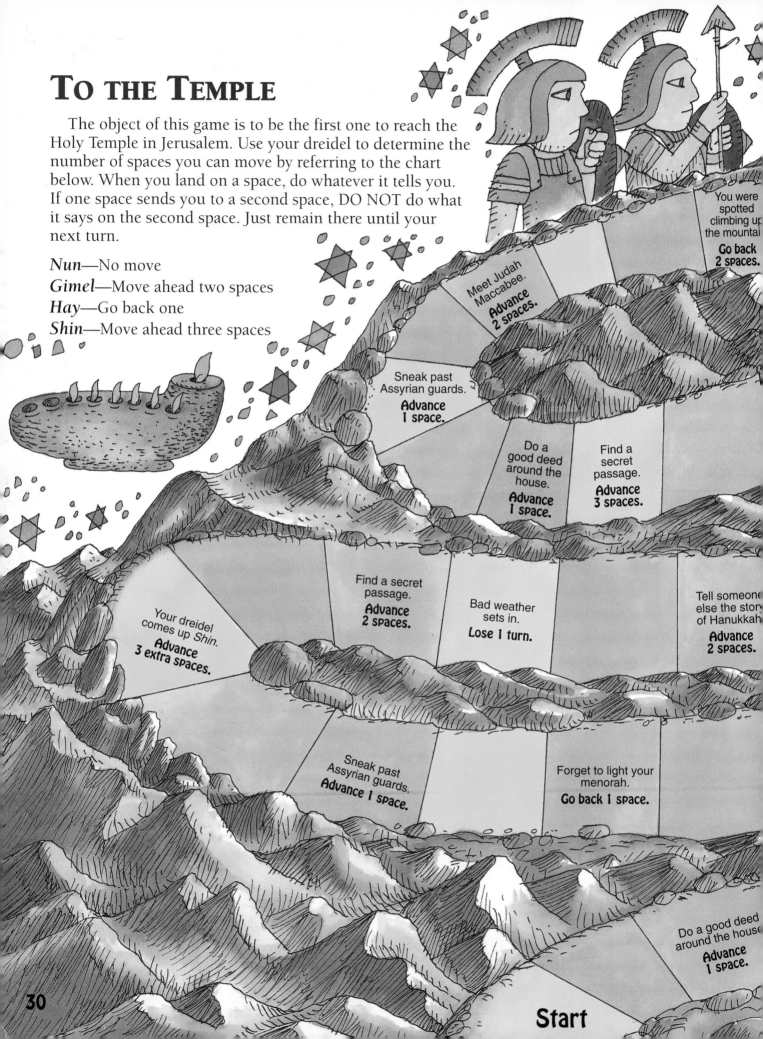

You were spotted climbing up the mountai[n]
Go back 2 spaces.

Meet Judah Maccabee.
Advance 2 spaces.

Sneak past Assyrian guards.
Advance 1 space.

Do a good deed around the house.
Advance 1 space.

Find a secret passage.
Advance 3 spaces.

Your dreidel comes up *Shin*.
Advance 3 extra spaces.

Find a secret passage.
Advance 2 spaces.

Bad weather sets in.
Lose 1 turn.

Tell someone else the story of Hanukkah
Advance 2 spaces.

Sneak past Assyrian guards.
Advance 1 space.

Forget to light your menorah.
Go back 1 space.

Do a good deed around the house
Advance 1 space.

Start

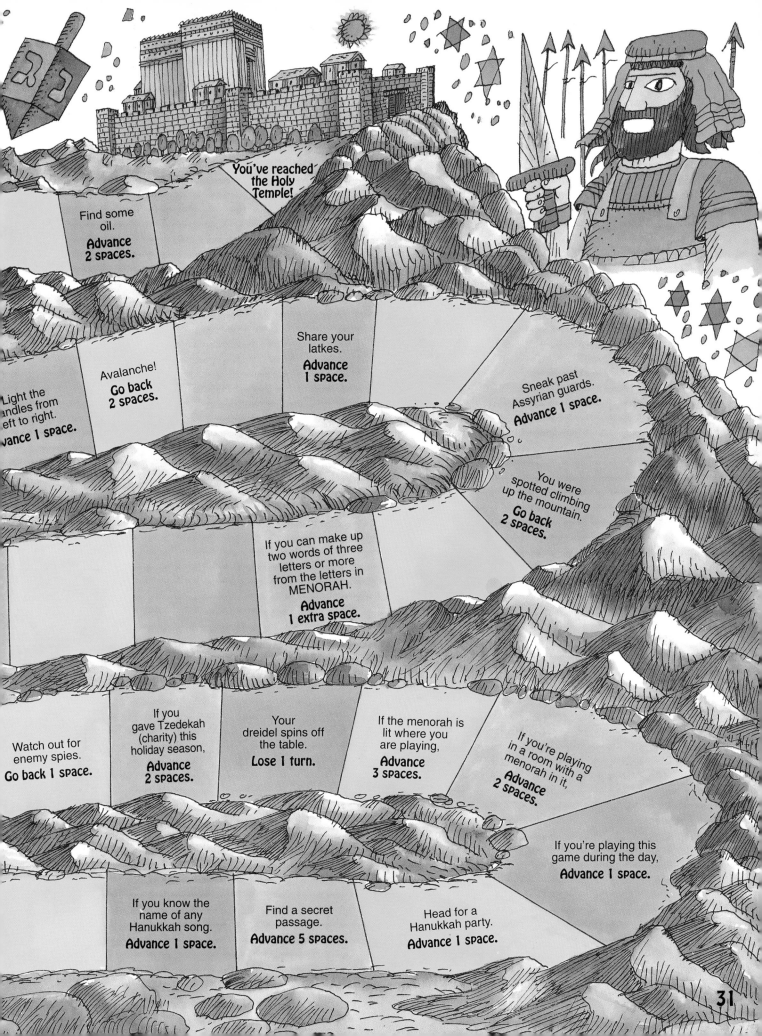

You've reached the Holy Temple!

Find some oil. **Advance 2 spaces.**

Light the candles from left to right. **Advance 1 space.**

Avalanche! **Go back 2 spaces.**

Share your latkes. **Advance 1 space.**

Sneak past Assyrian guards. **Advance 1 space.**

You were spotted climbing up the mountain. **Go back 2 spaces.**

If you can make up two words of three letters or more from the letters in MENORAH. **Advance 1 extra space.**

Watch out for enemy spies. **Go back 1 space.**

If you gave Tzedekah (charity) this holiday season, **Advance 2 spaces.**

Your dreidel spins off the table. **Lose 1 turn.**

If the menorah is lit where you are playing, **Advance 3 spaces.**

If you're playing in a room with a menorah in it, **Advance 2 spaces.**

If you're playing this game during the day, **Advance 1 space.**

If you know the name of any Hanukkah song. **Advance 1 space.**

Find a secret passage. **Advance 5 spaces.**

Head for a Hanukkah party. **Advance 1 space.**

A Hanukkah Story

Jeremy was unhappy. This was surprising since it was Hanukkah, a time for celebration. But the Festival of Lights did not bring much joy to Jeremy this year.

It had been snowing all day and school let out early. The bus dropped Jeremy off at the corner, where the pavement ended. He then trudged home through the swirling snow.

Sitting on a tray atop the table near the window were the menorah and candles. Soon the sun would go down, and that cold winter afternoon would get even darker.

Jeremy sulked his way into the kitchen, where his mother was working on dinner. She was cooking some latkes along with the regular meal. The oil bubbled like an overexcited aquarium, but even that noise didn't make Jeremy feel any better. Jeremy's mother saw how sad he was.

"What's wrong, honey?" she asked. "Don't you feel well?"

Jeremy sighed. "Do we have to celebrate Hanukkah?"

Jeremy's mother was a bit surprised. "But I thought you loved Hanukkah. Don't you like spinning the dreidel and playing games with Daddy and me?"

"This year is different. None of the other kids in my class celebrate Hanukkah. Why can't we have Christmas like they do?"

Jeremy's mother understood. She knew how difficult it was to move to a new place. Jeremy wanted to fit in, and he wanted the other kids to like him.

In the city where they had lived, there were a lot of other Jewish families. It was all right to celebrate Hanukkah, and people would accept that. But this year his father had gotten a new job, and the family had moved out to the country. They had left their big apartment and bought an old house. There were no streetlights, and they lived at the end of a dirt road.

Here in the country, there weren't many Jewish families. The people had Christmas pageants and Christmas dances and more—all of which were fine. No one in Jeremy's family minded any of this, and everyone in the community made sure that Jeremy and his family were invited to all the activites. It just made it a little tougher to be Jewish.

"How about we talk to your father when he gets home?" his mother asked.

"I guess." Jeremy slid off the chair and walked slowly into the living room.

The wind howled. It blew so hard that it shook the glass in the windows. Jeremy pulled back the curtain. Big clumps of white whipped through the darkness, coming down in a blanket. He couldn't recall ever having this much snow in the city.

"How is it out there?" Jeremy's mother came into the room, wiping her hands on her apron. "The radio says this is the worst storm of the season."

"I hope Dad's okay."

"I'm sure he is, honey. He'll be home soon."

The snow continued. Jeremy couldn't even see as far as the stump that he knew was right outside the window. The glass pane was cool against his head as he kept watch for his dad.

"Honey, let's light the menorah now."

"But you said we could talk to Dad first."

"We will," Mom said. "But it will make me feel better to have the candles burning until he gets home. All right?"

Jeremy shrugged. "I guess."

Mom lit the tallest candle as they recited the prayers together. Then Jeremy took the shammash. He watched closely as the light flared when the shammash was touched to the first candle. Jeremy had to admit that the glowing lights made him feel a little better.

A short while later, Jeremy was lying on the floor, reading a book. The menorah burned merrily in the window, the light of the two flames bouncing off the glass.

"Would you like to play with the dreidel?" Mom asked.

Jeremy shook his head.

"Well, how about a latke?"

"No, thank you. I just want this Hanukkah to be finished."

Just then they both heard someone banging on the front door. Jeremy and his mother ran to open it. There was Dad, covered with snow. He looked like a snowman come to life.

"Quick, let me in," Dad said. His breath huffed in and out as he beat his hands together to get warm. When Jeremy's mom pulled off Dad's coat, a pile of snow slid to the floor.

"Daddy, Daddy," Jeremy said. "I need to talk to you."

"Just a minute, sport." Dad's teeth chattered. "I've got to warm up. It's horrible outside."

"What happened?" asked Mom.

Dad took a deep breath. "All the roads are slick. It's snowing so hard I could barely see three feet in front of me. I couldn't go

more than a few miles an hour. Finally, I tried to stop where the pavement ends, but my car slid into the ditch. It's really stuck."

"It's a miracle you weren't hurt," Mom said.

"Well, I was able to get out and walk, but the wind and snow were just too much. I couldn't see at all, and then I fell into a snowbank. I was so cold I didn't think I was going to make it."

"But you did." Jeremy smiled.

"Yes, I did. And it was thanks to our menorah."

"What?" said Jeremy.

"I was stumbling around in the dark. I was afraid I was going to get lost. But then I saw the lights of our menorah flickering in the window."

"But how could that be?" Mom asked. "It's the first night and there are only two candles."

"It was enough," Dad said. "Maybe it was another Hanukkah miracle. Or maybe I was just lucky. Anyway, by the time I reached the door, I realized I had left my keys back in the car. So I had to knock."

With that, Dad gave Mom and Jeremy each a kiss.

"Dad, did you really see the menorah lights out there?"

Dad nodded. "I really did. Maybe I just wanted to see them, but I was so glad when I knew which house was ours."

Jeremy thought about that for a moment.

"Was there something else you wanted to ask me, sport?"

"Nothing," Jeremy said, happy that the lights of the menorah had brought his dad home. "I just wanted to wish you a Happy Hanukkah."

"Happy Hanukkah to you, Jeremy," his father said as they shared a big hug.

The Mouse Mitzvah
A Tale for Hanukkah

By Scott M. Drucker

Long ago in a village in Poland, there stood a wooden cottage so cozy and small that outstretched arms could almost touch opposite walls. In this cottage lived Rabbi Nathan, the oldest and wisest rabbi in the village, and his wife, Rachel.

It was wintertime. The winters in Poland are bitterly cold, and the animals had to find shelter wherever they could. The bears dug comfortable dens in shallow caves. The deer found shelter among the tall trees in the forests. The sparrows tried to keep warm by fluffing up their feathers until they resembled small balls of down. A lucky family of field mice found shelter in the eaves above the kitchen in the rabbi's cottage.

The mouse family consisted of a mother named Chana, a father named Mordechai, and their twin sons named Mazel and Tov. ("*Mazel tov*" means "congratulations" in Yiddish, the language spoken by Jews in Europe at that time.) The two mice were virtually identical except that each wore a different-colored yarmulke on his head so they could be told apart. Every morning Mordechai would place the yarmulkes on his sons' heads, reciting a prayer that said that just as the yarmulke sat above their heads so was God always above them. Mazel's yarmulke was dark blue, like the winter sky at night, and Tov's was dark green, like the tall fir trees that dotted the winter landscape.

One Hanukkah, Mazel and Tov were playing hide-and-seek near Rabbi Nathan's study. Several bearded men in long black coats had come to read from the Torah and to discuss important religious questions. The mice stood very still and listened to the conversation. Rabbi Nathan was saying, "The gift of *mitzvah* is the greatest gift anyone could give or receive." All the scholars agreed.

"What in the world is a *mitzvah*?" whispered Mazel to Tov. Hanukkah was a time for gifts, but here was a gift he knew nothing about.

"I have no idea," answered Tov.

Mazel thought for a moment. "Maybe it's a nice big plate of *kasha* with bow-tie noodles."

Tov nodded. "Or maybe it's a warm drawer full of socks."

"Let's ask Mama and Papa," they shouted together.

Chana and Mordechai knew several Yiddish words, but they had never heard of a *mitzvah*. "I have no idea what that word means," Papa answered, "but if Rabbi Nathan said it is the greatest gift, then who are we to question?" He and Mama were busily adding nuts and seeds to their winter supply.

This answer satisfied neither Mazel nor Tov. Tomorrow was the last day of Hanukkah, and they simply had to find out what a *mitzvah* was before Hanukkah was over. Mazel thought for a moment, then smiled. He and Tov would sneak into the bedroom late at night and ask the rabbi what a *mitzvah* was once and for all. Every mouse knew that humans always tell the truth when they are asleep.

A family of mice lived in the rabbi's cottage.

"What in the world is a mitzvah?"

opportunity to do a *mitzvah* for Hanukkah," said Tov. After asking their mother and father for permission, Mazel and Tov filled two small sacks with seeds and nuts that they skimmed off the top of their plentiful winter stash. Each mouse tied a sack to a twig and carried it on his back. They emptied their sacks on the barn floor, leaving a small pile of seeds and nuts for the hungry birds to eat.

The mice returned to their warm nest feeling much better about their own Hanukkah because they had helped someone else have a happy holiday as well. "The rabbi was right all along," they agreed. "A *mitzvah* really is the best gift of all."

A little later, Rabbi Nathan woke up. "The strangest vision came to me in a dream last night," he said to his wife. "Two mice asked me to explain to them what a *mitzvah* means."

"How ridiculous!" Rachel said, chuckling. And the two of them laughed and laughed until their attention turned toward the kitchen window, where a family of house sparrows were sitting on a branch, singing happily.

Late that night, Mazel and Tov climbed down the rafters to the curtains in the rabbi's bedroom. They shinnied down the curtains, leaped to the night table beside the rabbi's bed, and hopped to the rabbi's arm.

Slowly and carefully they crawled up to the rabbi's shoulder. They crept into the rabbi's long white beard. They clung to the rabbi's long curly sideburns with their tiny paws. Then they asked, "What exactly is a *mitzvah*? And how can we find one?"

Still sound asleep, the rabbi answered, "A *mitzvah* is not a thing; it is a good deed that someone does to help another. It is the greatest gift of all."

"*Oi vey!*" whispered Tov. "We were both wrong. A *mitzvah* is not a thing; it's a thing to do!"

That night Mazel and Tov climbed back to their nest in the eaves, which was filled with the pleasant, nutty aroma of seeds and acorns. They dreamed of a *mitzvah* to perform on the last day of Hanukkah.

The next morning, icy winds whipped around the rabbi's cottage. While the mice were warm and protected inside, a family of house sparrows living in the hay barn behind the cottage were freezing and hungry. A blizzard had covered the ground with a thick coat of snow.

"Mazel, this is the perfect

Now someone else would have a happy holiday.

Decorations and Gifts

Hanukkah is a time when family and friends have fun together. Some families exchange gifts on the first night or give little gifts each of the eight nights. However, Hanukkah isn't about giving presents. Those gifts are only symbols of the joy people feel at this time of the year. Being able to share such gifts in freedom is the real celebration of Hanukkah.

If people are coming to your home for the holiday, you may want to make your house look more festive. The warm lights of the menorah always make people happy, but here are some other decorations that may also brighten your home.

SPIRAL MOBILE

You need:

a paper plate, construction paper, scissors, thread

What to do:

1. Draw a spiral line on the plate and cut along the line, as shown. Then poke four pairs of holes in the spiral, placed as shown.

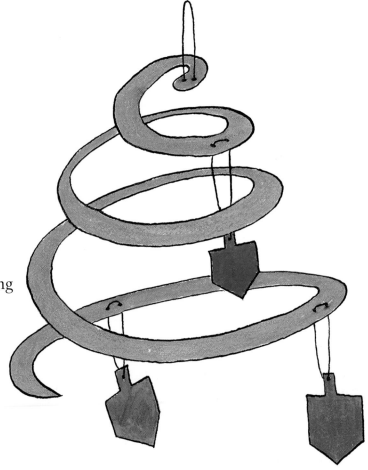

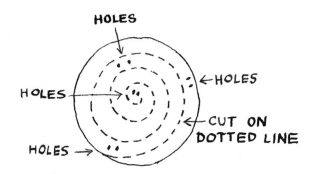

HOLES

HOLES →← HOLES

HOLES →

HOLES →

← CUT ON DOTTED LINE

3. Loop a piece of thread through each dreidel and pull the thread through a pair of holes on the spiral. Tie the ends.

2. Cut three small dreidels out of construction paper. Poke a hole in the top of each dreidel.

4. Tie a longer piece of thread through the pair of holes at the top of the mobile to hang it.

GLITTER MOBILE

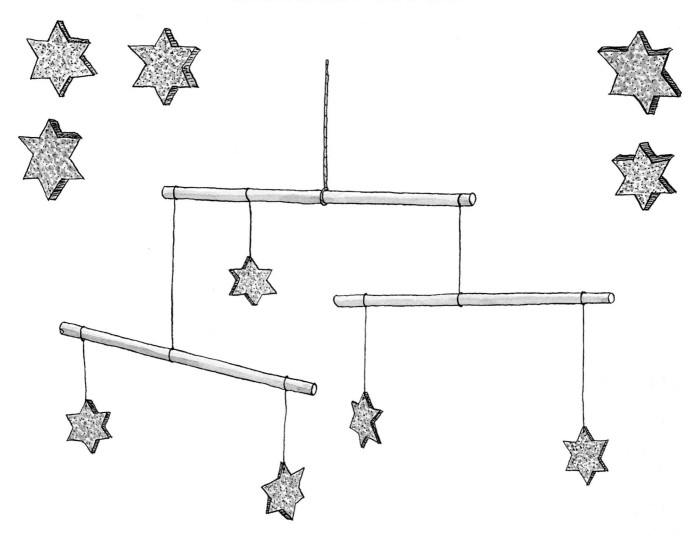

You need:

3 wooden rods or sticks, thread, cardboard, silver or gold glitter, scissors, glue

What to do:

1. Cut five Stars of David from cardboard. Poke a hole near the top of each one.

2. Spread glue on one side of each star and cover it with glitter. When the glue dries, cover the other side.

3. Loop a piece of thread through the hole in each star and tie the stars to the rods. Tie two rods to the ends of the third rod.

4. Hang the mobile from a loop attached to the middle of the third rod. You may have to move the rods and stars around to get the mobile to balance.

DREIDEL CHAIN

You will need:

a strip of gift wrap or colored paper, scissors, a ruler, a pen

What to do:

1. Cut a long strip of colored paper.

2. Divide the strip of paper into nine equal sections, using a pencil and ruler. Fold the paper along the pencil lines.

3. Draw a dreidel on the top of the paper. Keeping the paper folded, cut around only the top and bottom of the dreidel.

4. Unfold the paper, and print your greeting on each section, using words, letters, or a rebus. You might spell out Hanukkah, or you might put one of the menorah candles on each section. Use your own designs.

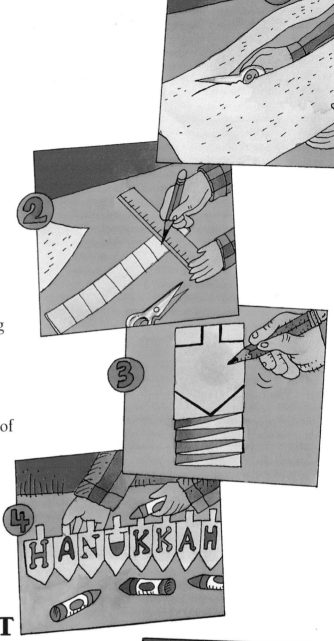

STAR OF DAVID PENDANT

You will need:

lightweight cardboard, aluminum foil, string

What to do:

1. Draw a small Star of David on a piece of lightweight cardboard. Cut out the shape.

2. Cover the front and back of the star with foil so that none of the cardboard shows.

3. Punch a hole at the top of the star. Thread a piece of string through the hole, and knot the ends so the pendant can hang around your neck.

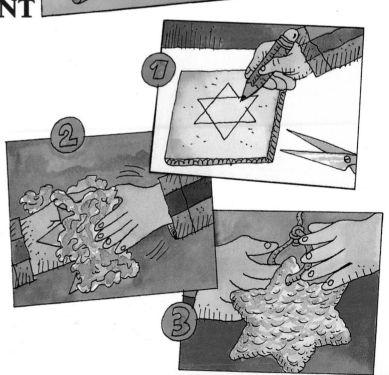

Spinning Stars

You will need:

two pieces of different-colored construction paper ($8\frac{1}{2}$" by 11"), white paper ($8\frac{1}{2}$" by 11"), thread or lightweight string, scissors, tape or glue

What to do:

1. Fold a piece of white paper in half. Draw one half of a large Star of David on the paper. Keep the center of the star on the folded edge of the paper.
2. Draw two more stars inside the larger star, following the pattern shown. Cut out these stars, trimming each one to be slightly smaller than the next. Be sure to maintain the shape of the Star of David.
3. Place the open star patterns on the construction paper, and trace around them. Cut out each star. You should have three stars: one large, one medium, and one small.
4. Line up the stars, one inside the next. Connect each star with a long piece of string or thread. Glue or tape the string in place. Use the loose end of the string to form a loop.
5. Hang the mobile away from a wall, and watch the stars spin.

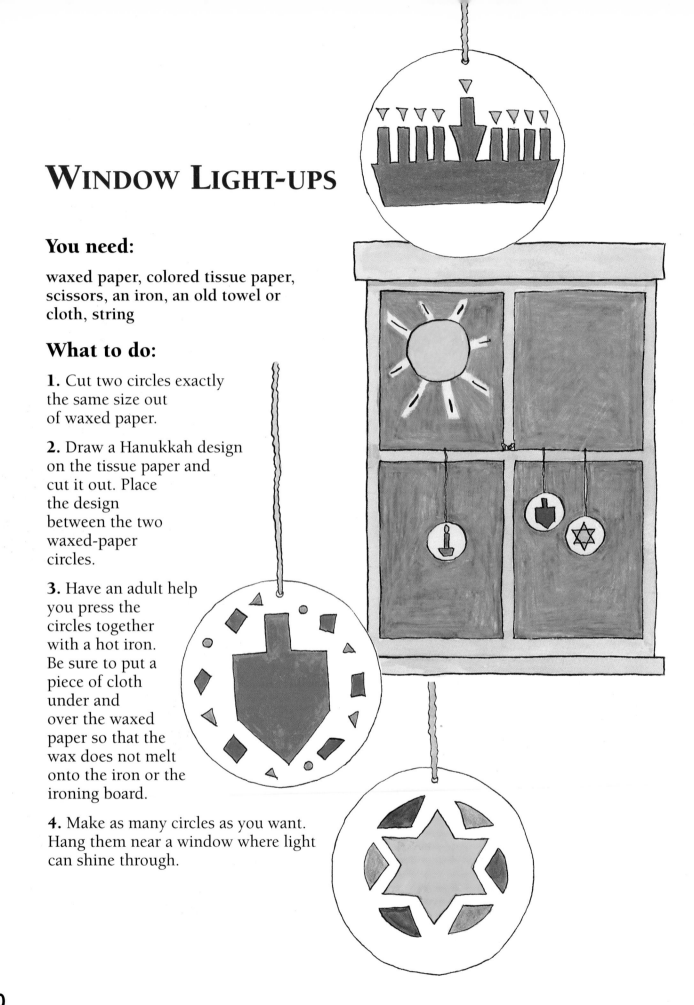

WINDOW LIGHT-UPS

You need:

waxed paper, colored tissue paper, scissors, an iron, an old towel or cloth, string

What to do:

1. Cut two circles exactly the same size out of waxed paper.

2. Draw a Hanukkah design on the tissue paper and cut it out. Place the design between the two waxed-paper circles.

3. Have an adult help you press the circles together with a hot iron. Be sure to put a piece of cloth under and over the waxed paper so that the wax does not melt onto the iron or the ironing board.

4. Make as many circles as you want. Hang them near a window where light can shine through.

Star of David Mobile

You need:

9 pipe cleaners or chenille sticks (12 inches long), strong scissors or wire cutters, thread

What to do:

1. Bend a pipe cleaner into the shape of a triangle, making the sides all the same length. Twist the ends together to close up the triangle.

2. Weave another pipe cleaner through the triangle, as shown, to make a Star of David.

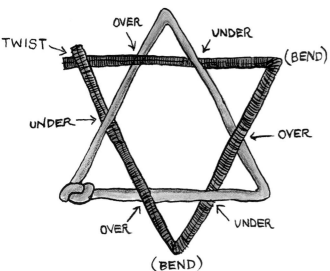

3. Cut a pipe cleaner in half and use the two pieces to make another star, following steps 1 and 2. Make two more small stars the same way.

4. Twist together the ends of two pipe cleaners to make one long one. Do this again to make a pair. Use the pair to repeat steps 1 and 2.

5. Hang the stars with thread, as shown. Tie a loop at the top to hang the mobile.

HANUKKAH CHAIN

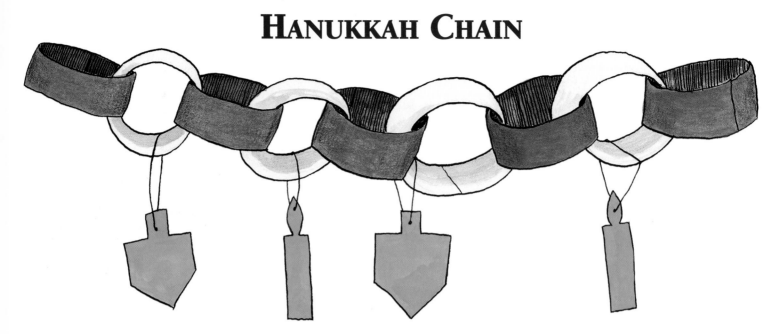

You need:

blue, yellow, and white construction paper, scissors, glue, thread

What to do:

1. Cut several strips of blue and white construction paper, each about 8 inches long and 1 inch wide.

2. Start with the blue strip. Glue the ends together to make a ring. Then loop a white strip through the ring and glue its ends together. Loop a blue strip through the white strip, and so on.

3. Cut Hanukkah shapes, such as dreidels and candles, from yellow construction paper. Poke a hole near the top of each shape. Use thread to hang the shapes from different links along the chain.

4. Make your chain as long as you wish. Hang it across a window sill or along a staircase. Can you make a chain long enough to go all the way around a room?

Hanukkah decorations are often made with the colors blue, white, and yellow. Blue and white are the colors of the Israeli flag. Yellow reminds us of the glow of the Hanukkah candles.

Cards and Gift Wrap

SPONGE DESIGNS

This idea can be used to create greeting cards or to make unique wrapping paper.

You will need: construction paper, a sponge, paint

What to do for a card:

1. Fold a piece of construction paper in half to form the card.
2. Cut a cellulose sponge into the shape of a Star of David.
3. Pour a small amount of paint onto a paper plate.
4. Dip the sponge into the paint so that one side of the star is completely covered. Press the wet sponge onto the card, arranging the stars in any design you like. When the paint is dry, write your message inside the card.

For wrapping paper:

Use colorful tissue paper to wrap your holiday gift box. Follow the instructions to the left, but put designs all over the wrapped gift box. Wait until the paint dries before giving this present to someone!

PAPER-PUNCH CARDS

You will need: two pieces of different-colored construction paper, a paper punch, glue

What to do:

1. Fold a piece of construction paper in half to form a card. Draw a holiday symbol on the front of the card.
2. Using a paper punch, make dots from construction paper. Glue the dots on top of the design.
3. Write a message inside.

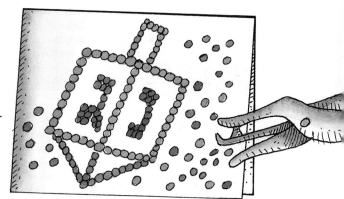

GLITTER MENORAH

You will need: construction paper, glue, glitter

What to do:

1. Fold the construction paper in half to form a card.
2. Draw a menorah on the front. Go over the lines of the menorah with glue.
3. Sprinkle on the glitter. Let the glue dry, and then shake off any extra glitter. Repeat the steps to add candles and flames. You might like to use different-colored glitter for each section.
4. Send the menorah as a greeting card. If you prefer, use the menorah as a decoration by standing the card on its open end.

MONOGRAMMED BOOKMARK

Here's an idea for an easy and inexpensive gift that can be personalized.

You will need:
a piece of thin cardboard (about 3" by 5"), clear adhesive paper, scissors

1. Fold the cardboard lengthwise to form a small card. Cut out a pattern similar to the one in the example. When done, you should be able to unfold the pattern and have a bookmark.
2. Decorate and add initials.
3. To keep the bookmark stiff and permanent, cover it with clear adhesive paper.

REBUS CARDS

Here's a way to make your Hanukkah cards even more fun. Include a rebus puzzle for the recipient to figure out. Rebus puzzles feature pictures that take the place of words and sounds. Some possibilities are illustrated below. See if you can figure out which Hanukkah word is represented by each rebus.

Cards

STAND-UP CARD

You need:

construction paper, scissors, glue, a marker or crayon

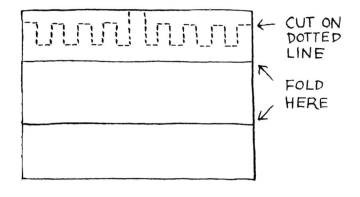

What to do:

1. Fold a sheet of construction paper into three sections, as shown. On the top section, drawn nine straight candle shapes, with the middle one higher than the others.

2. Cut out the candles. Cut flames from construction paper and glue them to the tops of the candles.

3. Print a greeting on the opposite section. Make sure you write it so that it will be right-side up when you fold up the section.

4. Give your card to someone to display on a shelf, table, or mantelpiece.

Do you have trouble remembering how to spell the word Hanukkah?
The most common ways to spell it are Hanukkah and Chanukah.
The Ch at the beginning of Chanukah is pronounced with a scraping sound from the back of your throat, the way it is said in Hebrew.

YARN CARD

You need:

white and yellow yarn, construction paper, scissors, glue

What to do:

1. Fold a sheet of construction paper in half. Draw a menorah on another piece and cut it out. Glue it to the front of the card.

2. Cut nine pieces of white yarn for the candles. Glue them onto the menorah. Cut little pieces of yellow yarn for the flames and glue them in place.

3. Write your Hanukkah greeting inside the card.

STRAW CARD

You need:

3 drinking straws, construction paper, scissors, glue

What to do:

1. Fold a sheet of construction paper in half.

2. Flatten the straws. Then cut each straw into two pieces of equal length. Arrange the pieces in the shape of a Star of David, and glue them to the front of the card.

3. Write your Hanukkah greeting inside the card.

PULL-OUT CARD

You need:

blue, white, and yellow construction paper, white ribbon, scissors, glue, a marker or crayon

What to do:

1. Draw a simple menorah shape on white construction paper and cut it out. Glue it to a sheet of blue construction paper.

2. Cut nine pieces of white ribbon. Glue them to the paper to make candles.

3. Above each candle, cut a hole shaped like a flame. To cut the hole, draw a flame with a pencil. Then, using pointed scissors, poke a hole in the middle of the flame and cut to the outside edges.

4. Cut a piece of yellow paper the same size as the blue sheet, but glue only along the top, bottom, and right-hand edges. Leave the left edge open.

5. Cut a narrow rectangle into the left edge. (Cut through both the yellow and blue sheets.)

6. Cut a rectangle out of blue paper slightly smaller than the blue and yellow sheets. On the left edge, glue a narrow strip of white paper with the word PULL written on it.

7. Slide the blue rectangle between the yellow and blue sheets of the card. The white PULL tab should line up with the rectangular hole on the left side of the card.

8. When the tab is pulled slowly to the left, the candles on the menorah will "light up." Decorate your special card with a Hanukkah greeting.

According to one legend, one of the first things the Maccabees did after they relit the Menorah and cleaned the Temple was to make new coins for the Jewish people. This may be how the tradition of giving gelt, or money, on Hanukkah was started.

GELT HOLDER

You need:

a plastic dish-detergent bottle, strong scissors, construction paper, rick-rack or yarn, glue

THROW THIS AWAY

DECORATE THIS

What to do:

1. Wash and dry the bottle. Cut out the bottom, as shown. (Soaking the bottle in warm water first will make this easier.)

2. Glue rick-rack or yarn around the edges. Cut Hanukkah shapes from construction paper and glue them to the plastic.

3. Give the holder as a gift, or keep it to hold your own Hanukkah gelt!

DREIDEL NOTE PAD

You need:

a stack of 3-inch-square sheets of white paper, colored construction paper, cardboard, yarn, glue, scissors

What to do:

1. Cut a dreidel shape out of cardboard, about four inches across and five inches long. Trace the dreidel shape onto construction paper and cut it out.

2. Glue the construction-paper dreidel onto the cardboard dreidel. Glue a piece of yarn around the edges to outline the dreidel.

3. Punch two holes at the top of the stack of white paper. Punch two holes the same distance apart at the top of the dreidel.

4. Line up the holes and tie the note pad in place with yarn. Write a Hanukkah greeting on the first sheet.

HANUKKAH JIGSAW PUZZLE

You need:

cardboard, crayons or markers, scissors, a small box

What to do.

1. Draw a Hanukkah scene on a piece of cardboard. Add a lot of details and colors.

2. Cut the cardboard into puzzle pieces with interesting shapes. Put the pieces in a box and give it to someone who enjoys working on puzzles.

STAR OF DAVID PICTURE FRAME

You need:

12 ice-cream sticks, a small photo of yourself, glue, glitter, construction paper, scissors, yarn

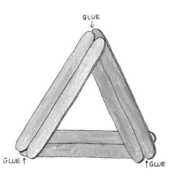

What to do:

1. Lay two ice-cream sticks side by side. Arrange two more pairs the same way. Glue the ends of each pair together to make a triangle. Make a second triangle the same way, then glue it onto the first to form a Star of David.

2. Spread glue on the star and cover it with glitter. Wait for it to dry.

3. Glue your photo to a piece of construction paper. Cut around the photo, leaving a 1-inch border. Glue the paper to the back of the star so that the photo shows through the middle. Trim away any extra paper that sticks out from behind.

4. Tie a loop of yarn at the top so that the person who receives your gift can hang it up.

In some families, children receive one gift on each night of Hanukkah. In other families, all of the gifts are exchanged on the first night.

HANUKKAH PLACE MATS

You need:

4 pieces of heavy cloth (about 12" by 18" each), extra scraps of cloth, scissors, a 2-inch-square piece of cardboard, yarn, a sewing needle, thread

What to do:

1. Pull threads from around the edges of each large piece of cloth to make fringe borders.

2. Cut four cloth dreidel shapes, about 5 inches across and 5 inches tall.

3. Sew the sides and bottoms of each dreidel to the bottom left-hand corner of each mat, using the simple running stitch shown. Leave the top edge of each dreidel open to create a pocket for the silverware and napkin.

RUNNING STITCH

4. Make tassels to attach to the corners of each place mat. To make a tassel, wrap a long piece of yarn several times around a 2-inch cardboard square. Slip a smaller piece of yarn between the loops and the cardboard, then tie tightly to bunch up the yarn, as shown. Remove the cardboard and tie another piece of yarn just below the first tie, as shown. Cut through the loops. Sew the tassel to the cloth with a needle and thread.

WRAP YARN

← TIE

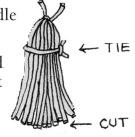

← TIE

← CUT

5. Roll up each place mat and tie with yarn. Present this gift set to someone special.

Delicious Latke Recipes

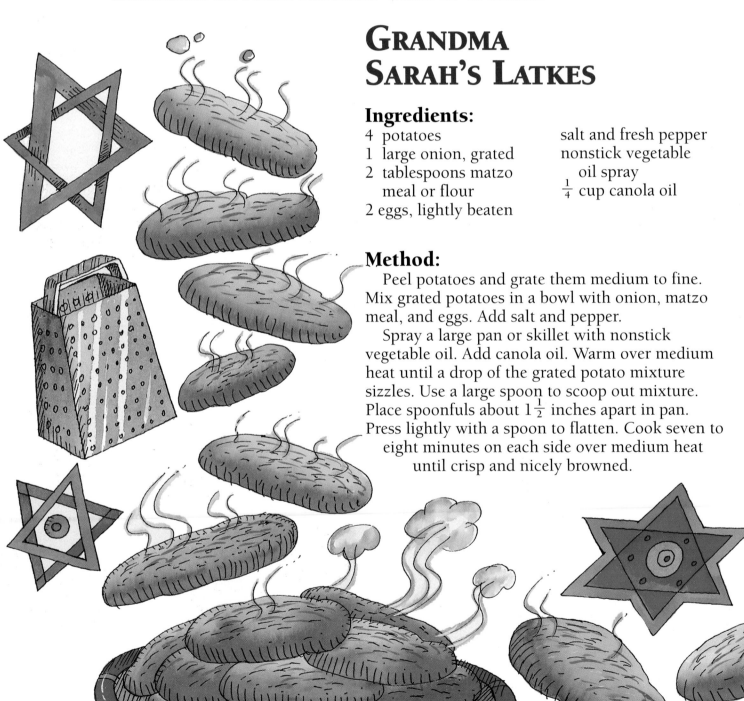

Be very careful when attempting these recipes. To get the true "flavor" of the holiday, latkes should be cooked in oil, which symbolizes the oil from the Temple. However, to cook just right, the oil must be VERY HOT. DO NOT attempt to make latkes without some help from a grown-up.

These recipes all come from Grandma Sarah's kitchen. Though I tried to approximate the measurements needed for each recipe, Grandma's favorite measurement was a *bissel*. This means "a little bit" in Yiddish.

GRANDMA SARAH'S LATKES

Ingredients:

4 potatoes
1 large onion, grated
2 tablespoons matzo
  meal or flour
2 eggs, lightly beaten

salt and fresh pepper
nonstick vegetable
  oil spray
$\frac{1}{4}$ cup canola oil

Method:

Peel potatoes and grate them medium to fine. Mix grated potatoes in a bowl with onion, matzo meal, and eggs. Add salt and pepper.

Spray a large pan or skillet with nonstick vegetable oil. Add canola oil. Warm over medium heat until a drop of the grated potato mixture sizzles. Use a large spoon to scoop out mixture. Place spoonfuls about $1\frac{1}{2}$ inches apart in pan. Press lightly with a spoon to flatten. Cook seven to eight minutes on each side over medium heat until crisp and nicely browned.

SWEET POTATO LATKES

Ingredients:
4 sweet potatoes
2 eggs, lightly beaten
2 tablespoons matzo meal or flour
1 tablespoon sugar
a bissel (little bit) salt
$\frac{1}{2}$ cup raisins
nonstick vegetable oil spray
$\frac{1}{4}$ cup canola oil

Method:
Peel potatoes and grate them fine. Mix gratings in a bowl with flour or matzo meal and eggs. Add salt, sugar, and raisins. (After mixing, the batter will seem a bit looser than that in the potato latke recipe.)

Spray a large pan or skillet with nonstick vegetable oil. Add canola oil. Warm over medium head until a drop of the grated mixture sizzles. Use a large spoon to scoop out mixture. Place spoonfuls about $1\frac{1}{2}$ inches apart in pan. Press lightly with a spoon to flatten. Cook seven to eight minutes on each side over medium heat until crisp and nicely browned.

NON-POTATO LATKES

Ingredients:
$\frac{1}{2}$ cup matzo meal
$\frac{3}{4}$ teaspoon salt
$\frac{3}{4}$ cup cold water
3 eggs
nonstick vegetable oil spray

Method:
Mix all ingredients in a bowl. Allow mixture to stand for 30 minutes. Spray skillet or pan with nonstick vegetable oil, and place on high heat. When the pan is hot, use a large spoon to scoop out mixture. Place spoonfuls about $1\frac{1}{2}$ inches apart in pan. Brown on both sides.

TOPPINGS

One important part of the latke that you shouldn't overlook is the topping. Some people prefer sour cream or butter. However, applesauce is by far the favorite latke topping in most homes. For non-potato latkes, favorite toppings include either applesauce, honey, or fruit jelly.

Many foods are linked with particular holidays. Hamentashen goes with Purim, matzah goes with Passover, and latkes go with Hanukkah. Yet there are other foods that also go with Hanukkah.

Tzimmes (SIM-iss) is a cooked dish of carrots and fruits, such as pineapple or prunes. There is a usually a sweet glaze that makes this dish taste better than it may sound. The carrots are cooked in oil, as are most Hanukkah foods. Tzimmes is usually served as one of the vegetable portions of the meal.

One idea of why Tzimmes is linked to Hanukkah is that the pieces of sliced carrot resemble the Hanukkah gelt coins that are given to children.

Sfganiyout are special Hanukkah jelly-filled doughnuts. There are many ways to spell and pronounce the name of this sweet treat. One way is souf-GANI-yot. In my house, we usually said "Souffy." These donuts are deep-fried in oil, then coated with sugar or cinnamon, before adding the jelly.

CHOCOLATE

Most Jewish holidays recall the difficult times of history. There is usually a reference to the hardships that were endured by our ancestors. Yet at the end of every meal, we always add some kind of sweet. One reason we do this is to symbolize our hope for a "sweet" and pleasant future.

In cakes, cookies, and coins, chocolate is one sweet we all enjoy.

APPLESAUCE

This may be the all-time champion of latke toppings. You can easily buy kosher applesauce, but it's also fun to make.

Here's one easy recipe:

Ingredients:

4 pounds ripe baking apples
1 lemon
$\frac{1}{2}$ cup of apple cider or juice
honey or sugar
cinnamon candies, like Red Hots

Cut the apples and lemon into quarters. Put them all in a big pot. Mix in the candies, along with the apple cider. Cover the pot and bring the cider to a boil. Simmer over a low flame, stirring once in a while to keep the apples from sticking. Add more cider if needed. Cook about twenty minutes or until apples are soft. Let cool.

Run the soft apples through a food processor. Adjust the flavor with honey or sugar. Refrigerate until served.

Hanukkah Hidden Pictures

In the large picture find the book, pencil, mouse, boomerang, butterfly, flag, fork, magnet, hat, leaf, dragonfly, banana, horn, sickle, and eyeglasses.

Puzzles and Jokes

NAME CHANGE

Judah Maccabee led the Jews against the forces of King Antiochus. To discover the meaning of the name Maccabee, follow the directions at each step. If you go through carefully, you should be able to come up with the right answer.

MACCABEE

Change the first pair of letters into a pair of M's: _____

Change the last vowel into the eighteenth letter of the alphabet: _____

Change the first M into the letter that appears at both ends of the name of this holiday: _____

Somewhere in this newest word, the first two letters of the alphabet appear next to one another. Remove both: _____

Judah Maccabee was known as "The _____."

LIGHTHEARTED

Hanukkah is all about lights. To join in the fun, see if you can identify each "light" word. Then put the correct letters in the corresponding spaces to learn Hanukkah's nickname. We put in some of the letters to get you started.

1. A set of stairs: ___ light
　　　　　　　　　　1

2. Slim or flimsy: ___ light
　　　　　　　　　　3

3. Accompanies thunder: light ___ ___ ___ ___
　　　　　　　　　　　　　　　　　　4

4. This guides ships into harbor: light ___ ___ ___ ___ ___
　　　　　　　　　　　　　　　　　　　　　　　2

5. In England this is called a torch, even though it uses batteries: ___ ___ ___ ___ ___ light
　　　　　　　　　　　　　　　　6　5

Hanukkah is called the
___ ___ ___ T ___ V ___ ___ of lights.
　1　 2　 3　　 4　　5　 6

HANUKKAH HA-HA'S

What were Judah Maccabee's famous words that began the holiday of Hanukkah?"

"Anybody got a light?"

Where do baby Hanukkah tops sleep?

In the dreidel cradle.

HANUKKAH WORD SEARCH

In the letters below, look across, down, backward, or diagonally to find all the words that have to do with Hanukkah. You can do this puzzle without even writing in the book, either by looking or by putting a piece of tracing paper over the puzzle before you circle any words.

Apple
Candle
December
Dreidel
Eight
Gelt
Gift
Gimel
Hay
Honey
Israel
Kislev
Latke
Light
Maccabee
Menorah
November
Nun
Oil
Peace
Po
Shammash
Shin
Song
Toy

```
              I
           Y  N  S
        A  P  U  H  R
     H  Q  K  N  A  F  A
  R  E  B  M  E  V  O  N  M  P  C  E  O  P  L
  E  K  I  S  L  E  V  M  E  A  G  L  I
     B  J  E  L  P  P  A  A  N  N  O
        M  S  H  I  N  S  C  D  O
     I  Y  E  N  O  H  H  E  L  S  R
  G  M  A  C  C  A  B  E  E  E  E  Z  A
  G  E  L  T  G  T  E  L  E  D  I  E  R  D  H
     H  I  O  D  W  G  K
        G  F  Y  H  T
           I  T  A
              L
```

HANUKKAH MAZE

See if you can find one path that leads to the menorah.
Try to pick up all eight candles on the way without
crossing back over any single path.

58

Hanukkah Songs

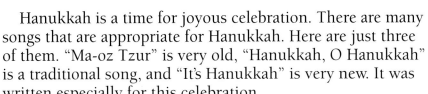

Hanukkah is a time for joyous celebration. There are many songs that are appropriate for Hanukkah. Here are just three of them. "Ma-oz Tzur" is very old, "Hanukkah, O Hanukkah" is a traditional song, and "It's Hanukkah" is very new. It was written especially for this celebration.

IT'S HANUKKAH!

Lyrics and music by Allen and Gruskin

Verse 1

When Ju - dah Mac - ca - bee re - cap - tured the tem - ple, he found just a lit - tle pot of oil. But God did not re - fuse the pray'rs of the an - cient Jews and gave them the light by which to toil.

Chorus

It's Ha - nuk - kah a - gain! Won't you come on in? No mat - ter who may win, we'll let the drei - del spin. This Fes - ti - val of Lights, the can - dles burn so bright. We light the sham - mash to help re - mind us it's Ha - nuk - kah to - night!

Verse 2

The oil lasted for eight days
And so God's name we praise
During this festival of lights.

The miracle that happened there
Gave us a light to share
Through even the darkest of our nights.
Repeat Chorus

MA-OZ TZUR
(Rock of Ages) *Arranged by Dan Fox*

Ma - oz tzur y' - shu a tee, L' - cha na - eh L'-sha - bey - ach.

Tee - kon beyt t' - fee - la - tee, V' - sham to - dah n' - za - bey - ach. L' -

eyt ta - chin mat - bey - ach Mee - tzar ham' - na bey - ach,

Az eg - mor b' - shir miz - mor Cha - nu - kat ha - miz - bey - ach.

Az eg - mor b' - shir miz - mor Cha - nu - kat ha - miz - bey - ach.

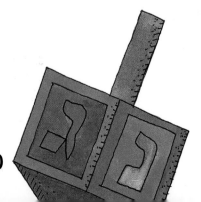

Rock of ages, let our song
Praise Thy saving power.
Thou amidst the raging foes
Wast our sheltering tower.
Furious they assailed us,
But Thine arm availed us.
(And Thy word broke their sword
When our own strength failed us.) *2 times*

HANUKKAH, O HANUKKAH

Arranged by Steve Gruskin

Traditional

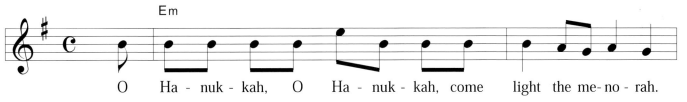

O Ha - nuk - kah, O Ha - nuk - kah, come light the me - no - rah.

Let's have a par - ty, we'll all dance the ho - rah. Ga - ther round the ta - ble; we'll

give you a treat. Shi - ny tops to play with and lat - kes to eat. And while we are

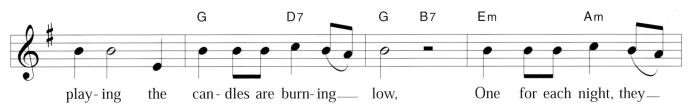

play - ing the can - dles are burn - ing___ low, One for each night, they___

shed a sweet light To re - mind us of days so long a - go.

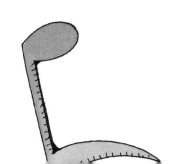

61

Words to Remember

dreidel (DRAY dul)

A four-sided spinning top or the game played with it. The top has the Hebrew letters נ, ג, ה, and ש on it. The letters stand for Hebrew words that mean "A great miracle happened there." In Israel, the last letter is a פ instead of a ש. The פ stands for the Hebrew word for "here."

gelt (GELT)

A Yiddish word meaning "money," given to children on Hanukkah.

gimel (GIM el)

A Hebrew letter, ג, that sounds like the g in good. It is one of the four letters that appear on all dreidels.

Hanukkah (HAHN oo kah)

The Hebrew word for "rededication." It is the name given to the eight-day holiday that celebrates the cleansing of the Holy Temple after it was ruined by the army of Antiochus.

hanukkiyah (hahn oo KEY uh)

A menorah or candelabrum used specifically and solely for Hanukkah.

hay (HAY)

A Hebrew letter, ה, that makes the h sound. It is one of the four letters that appear on all dreidels.

Judah Maccabee (JOO duh MAK uh bee)

The solider who led his small army against the troops of Antiochus, driving them from Jerusalem and saving the Holy Temple. The name Maccabee, which means "hammer," was given to Judah for the powerful blows he struck for freedom.

latke (LAHT kuh)

A Yiddish word for "pancake" and the special potato pancakes fried in oil and eaten on Hanukkah.

menorah (meh NOR uh)

A candleholder or oil lamp with many branches. During Hanukkah, a menorah with nine branches (one taller than the other eight) is lit on each night.

nun (NUN)

A Hebrew letter, ‏נ‎, that makes the *n* sound. It is one of the four letters that appear on all dreidels.

peh (PAY)

A Hebrew letter, ‏פ‎, that makes the *p* sound. It is one of the four letters that appear on a dreidel in Israel.

shammash (SHAH mush)

A Hebrew word meaning "servant." On the Hanukkah menorah, the shammash is the tallest candle. It is used to light the other candles. It is usually in the middle or at one end of the menorah.

shin (SHEEN)

A Hebrew letter, ‏ש‎, that makes the *sh* sound. It is one of the four letters that appear on a dreidel, except in Israel, where a peh (‏פ‎) appears instead.

tzedekah (Tseh DUCK ah)

The act of giving charity.

ANSWERS

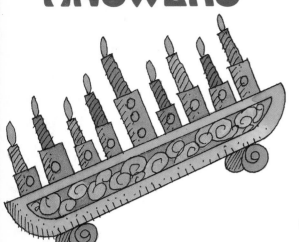

PAGES 30-31

In the game, you might land on the space calling for you to make words from the letters in MENORAH. Here are forty words. You may have found others.

are, arm, ear, earn, enamor, eon, era, ham, hare, harem, harm, hear, hem, hen, her, hoe, home, homer, hone, horn, man, mane, mare, mean, men, moan, more, name, near, nor, omen, one, ore, ram, ran, ream, rhea, roam, roan, Roman

PAGE 55

These are the objects hidden in the picture

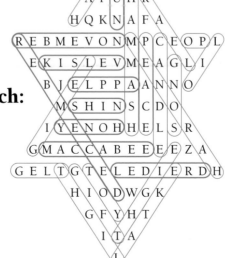

PAGE 44

Rebus Cards:
1. Happy 2. Menorah 3. Dreidel 4. Latke
5. Hanukkah 6. Winter 7. Candles

Letter:
Dear Tony,
I just wanted to wish you a Happy Hanukkah!
 Your friend,
 Carl

PAGE 56

Lighthearted:
1. flight
2. slight
3. lightning
4. lighthouse
5. flashlight
Hanukkah is called the festival of lights.

Name Change:
MAMMABEE
MAMMABER
HAMMABER
HAMMER

PAGE 57:

Hanukkah Word Search:

PAGE 58:

Hanukkah Maze: